I0584523

Zelda at the Oasis

P. H. Lin

A Samuel French Acting Edition

SAMUELFRENCH.COM
SAMUELFRENCH-LONDON.CO.UK

Copyright © 2015 by P. H. Lin
All Rights Reserved

ZELDA AT THE OASIS is fully protected under the copyright laws of the United States of America, the British Commonwealth, including Canada, and all other countries of the Copyright Union. All rights, including professional and amateur stage productions, recitation, lecturing, public reading, motion picture, radio broadcasting, television and the rights of translation into foreign languages are strictly reserved.

ISBN 978-0-573-70305-8

www.SamuelFrench.com
www.SamuelFrench-London.co.uk

FOR PRODUCTION ENQUIRIES

UNITED STATES AND CANADA
Info@SamuelFrench.com
1-866-598-8449

UNITED KINGDOM AND EUROPE
Plays@SamuelFrench-London.co.uk
020-7255-4302

Each title is subject to availability from Samuel French, depending upon country of performance. Please be aware that *ZELDA AT THE OASIS* may not be licensed by Samuel French in your territory. Professional and amateur producers should contact the nearest Samuel French office or licensing partner to verify availability.

CAUTION: Professional and amateur producers are hereby warned that *ZELDA AT THE OASIS* is subject to a licensing fee. Publication of this play(s) does not imply availability for performance. Both amateurs and professionals considering a production are strongly advised to apply to Samuel French before starting rehearsals, advertising, or booking a theatre. A licensing fee must be paid whether the title(s) is presented for charity or gain and whether or not admission is charged. Professional/ Stock licensing fees are quoted upon application to Samuel French.

No one shall make any changes in this title(s) for the purpose of production. No part of this book may be reproduced, stored in a retrieval system, or transmitted in any form, by any means, now known or yet to be invented, including mechanical, electronic, photocopying, recording, videotaping, or otherwise, without the prior written permission of the publisher. No one shall upload this title(s), or part of this title(s), to any social media websites.

For all enquiries regarding motion picture, television, and other media rights, please contact Samuel French.

MUSIC MATERIALS

A digital sound file package for *ZELDA AT THE OASIS*, which includes tracks of the piano playing sequences as well as files of other sound design elements used in the New York production are available as a downloadable product through samuelfrench.com. This digital sound file package is intended for licensed performances of *ZELDA AT THE OASIS* only. Please contact your Theatrical Specialist for further information regarding the purchase and use of this digital sound file package.

MUSIC USE NOTE

Licensees are solely responsible for obtaining formal written permission from copyright owners to use copyrighted music in the performance of this play and are strongly cautioned to do so. If no such permission is obtained by the licensee, then the licensee must use only original music that the licensee owns and controls. Licensees are solely responsible and liable for all music clearances and shall indemnify the copyright owners of the play(s) and their licensing agent, Samuel French, against any costs, expenses, losses and liabilities arising from the use of music by licensees. Please contact the appropriate music licensing authority in your territory for the rights to any incidental music.

IMPORTANT BILLING AND CREDIT REQUIREMENTS

If you have obtained performance rights to this title, please refer to your licensing agreement for important billing and credit requirements.

ZELDA AT THE OASIS opened Off Broadway at St. Luke's Theatre on December 4, 2012. The production was directed by Andy Sandberg, with scenic design by Colin McGurk, costume design by Dustin Cross, lighting design by Grant Yeager, sound design by Daniel Melnick, choreography by Elisabetta Spuria, and casting by Michael Cassara. The general press representative was Susan L. Schulman, and the general manager was Jessimeg Productions/Edmund Gaynes. The production stage manager was Shelby Taylor Love. The cast for the New York premiere was as follows:

ZELDA. . . . . Gardner Reed
BAR MAN . . . . Edwin Cahill

ZELDA AT THE OASIS was originally presented by Venus Theatre Company in Laurel, Maryland.

CHARACTERS

ZELDA – (1900-1948) The wife of F. Scott Fitzgerald. A strikingly pretty woman, in her early thirties. Zelda was a Southern Belle who was gifted in writing, and painting, and also in the dance. All she desired was to be recognized, in her own right, for her talents and for her accomplishments in these fields.

BAR MAN A bartender and "Piano Man." No older than Zelda. He is youthful in both attitude and appearance. This character also plays all of the other roles in this piece, male as well as female.

SETTING

An after hours club, "The Oasis"
Somewhere in New York City

TIME

The early 1930s

PLAYWRIGHT'S NOTES ABOUT
ZELDA AND SCOTT FITZGERALD

Zelda and Scott Fitzgerald were one of the most fabled and recognizable celebrity couples throughout the world during the decade with which they are most associated...the Roaring 1920s. They were beautiful, seemingly wealthy, reckless and young.

With the publication of his first novel, *This Side of Paradise* (1920), Scott was hailed as one of America's most promising young authors. He had access to both money, and the chance to become part of the elite and extravagant NY society to which he had always aspired. With Zelda as his partner, the two found ready acceptance in the endless parties and excesses that defined the Jazz Age.

Zelda Sayre was a Belle from a prominent though not necessarily a wealthy family in Montgomery, Alabama. Her father was a judge. Her mother was a home-maker whose own artistic aspirations had been quashed.

Since the Sayres came from Southern aristocracy, Zelda could take shelter in her family's reputation and remain above reproach. She could also run wild...which she did on every occasion.

Zelda longed to be acclaimed for her talents as well as her antics. Eventually she became a published novelist, a produced playwright, an artist with work shown in galleries, and a ballet dancer with a contract to perform with the San Carlo Opera Ballet in Italy.

Zelda and Scott met at a country club dance in 1917. Scott had been stationed at Camp Sheridan outside of Zelda's home town, in anticipation of being sent off to fight in WWI. Zelda was barely out of high school.

A whirlwind courtship punctuated by fights and a prolonged break-up ensued. They married in 1920 (once he had sufficient funds from his book to support her). He was twenty-four. She was still nineteen. Their only child (Frances Scott Fitzgerald) was born in 1921.

Despite Scott's early success, their extravagant party lifestyle, coupled with an ill-fated attempt for Scott to become a playwright, had its consequences. By 1923, Fitzgerald was forced to write his way out of debt by taking on short story commissions for "magazine fillers." Personal and professional distractions kept him from making progress on his third novel, *The Great Gatsby*.

Scott became a confirmed alcoholic. There were frequent domestic rows. Literary opinion makers stopped considering Fitzgerald a serious author because of his playboy reputation. Under intense strain from the increasingly failing marriage, Zelda experienced the onset of an hereditary predisposition…the bi-polar condition which would plague her for the rest of her life.

Seeking tranquility for both, Zelda and Scott, along with their daughter Scottie, moved to Paris in 1924. There the couple assumed a prominent place among expatriate socialites and artists of the Lost Generation…the most notable of whom was Ernest Hemingway.

France proved not to be a solution to their myriad of problems. The marriage became a tangle of jealousy, resentment and acrimony. Zelda became obsessed with having a career as a ballerina, and practiced to exhaustion. In 1930, she had the first of her many nervous breakdowns. Although Scott and Zelda remained married, the couple rarely lived together after her 1932 breakdown. He did provide for her care until his death in 1940.

Zelda died eight years later (1948) in a fire at a sanitarium in Asheville, NC. She and Scott are buried in St. Mary's Catholic Church in Rockville, MD.

1

(The scene: An after hours club, "The Oasis." Somewhere in New York City. The time: the early 1930s.)

(At rise: **BAR MAN** *is busy wiping down the bar, part of his process for "closing down for the night.")*

(In addition to the bar, the room contains a few small tables and chairs. A battered upright piano at the edge of a small dance floor completes the setting. The room is in disarray, cluttered with items left behind by previous patrons.)

*(***ZELDA FITZGERALD**, *wife of the noted American novelist F. Scott Fitzgerald, a drink in her hand, dances to the song "**GIRL OF MY DREAMS**." She sings its tune to herself as she dances alone.)*

ZELDA. Are you catching all this, Jelly Bean?

BAR MAN. Hard not to.

ZELDA. Well, good. I like being noticed.

(She flashes a smile, as she undulates to the bar, lounges across it, and pushes her empty glass in **BAR MAN** *'s direction.)*

So, you gonna re-fill my spirit? With 200 percent proof of your love and adoration.

BAR MAN. You've had enough.

ZELDA. Me? Never! Never enough! Oh, relax, Sugar Plum. Getting "blotto" is not a weakness from which I suffer. So make it sloe, and gin, and heavy on the fizz.

(a beat)

What's keeping you? Fill'er up!

BAR MAN. Sorry, Darlin', the party's over. The booze is capped for the night.

ZELDA. But I'm not ready to leave.

BAR MAN. Your problem. Not mine.

ZELDA. You'd throw me out? Before I've figured out what place to be calling my home?

(**BAR MAN** *sets a cup of coffee before her.*)

What's this?

BAR MAN. Cup of Joe. Clear your head.

ZELDA. Head is fine, Jelly Bean. It's the soul that's feeling fuzzy.

(**BAR MAN** *ignores her. He continues to clean.*)

Have you any idea who I am?

BAR MAN. Not a clue.

ZELDA. I am all things new and modern!

BAR MAN. If I had a nickel for every dame who thinks that.

ZELDA. I don't think. I do. I swim in fountains. I dance upon tabletops.

BAR MAN. Not in here you don't.

ZELDA. I stop traffic when I ride on the hoods of taxis!

BAR MAN. A regular good time girl.

ZELDA. No regular. An original and damn proud!

BAR MAN. It's time you called it a night.

ZELDA. You really don't recognize me?

BAR MAN. I recognize you're out way past your bedtime.

ZELDA. Want to put me to bed?

BAR MAN. Not tonight. I got plans already.

ZELDA. Hell's bells! You're no fun.

(*He sets a cup of coffee in front of her.*)

BAR MAN. Drink this coffee, Darlin'. You need it.

ZELDA. I'll give you a hint. I'm the girl who put the "flap" into flapper.

BARMAN. You don't look like Clara Bow.

ZELDA. I am not some Hollywood hussy. No, Sugar, I'm Zelda. Zelda Fitzgerald. The wife of F. Scott?

(no response)

BAR MAN. The writer? He's dead.

ZELDA. Artistically, maybe. But no. My husband is just as alive and kicking as I am.

BAR MAN. Then what is it I'm remembering? Six...maybe seven years ago. Front page of *The Herald.* A hospital. No. A loony bin. Yeah, that was it! Only that photo wasn't of him. That was of you!

ZELDA. I have never been confined. If I've ever entered a *clinic,* and I have...many times...I've done so of my own accord. I sign myself in for some rest and recuperation. And when the spirit is sufficiently renewed? Then I sign myself right back out!

(She smells the coffee.)

Um. Strong. But strong enough to keep me buoyed up? To save me from this tow that keeps dragging me under?

(a beat)

Ah, forget it! Forget about decisions you can't control. Just focus on those you can. Like should I keep pinning my hopes on Scott...or resign myself to signing myself in again. Inside I can count on a whole raft of support... and a chaise to lounge back on like so.

(She leans back on the chair, slips off her shoes, and puts her feet up on a second chair, lounging.)

Inside I'm encouraged...supported...to discover my own sweet rhythms in my own sweet rhymes.

(She closes her eyes.)

*(**BAR MAN** finds a pair of wire-rim glasses and transforms into **DOCTOR**. They are in a garden at the sanitarium.)*

DOCTOR. Well, if you are not the picture of perfect health today, Mrs. Fitzgerald.

ZELDA. And all because of you, Doctor, and your staff! At your Institute my fancies simply flower! Florabundi!

DOCTOR. How lovely. Then our cure appears to be working.

ZELDA. You are such a relief. And this place is such a respite!

DOCTOR. I am pleased. Gratified.

ZELDA. *(She totally relaxes.)* But an artist worth salt can't stay inside forever. She has to go out and engage where the real talents thrive. And so I shall, once my spirit is renewed.

(ZELDA moves back onto the dance floor. She begins to dance while she hums "GIRL OF MY DREAMS.")

(She moves seamlessly, with confidence, and flair. Although dancing alone, she exudes a radiance. But then, after all, ZELDA is a dancer, and comfortable when it comes to using her body as a means of expression.)

(BAR MAN, having transformed back into himself, is totally disgusted.)

BAR MAN. Of all of the bars in all of New York, why this one?

ZELDA. Your curve appealed. In the palm tree sign outside. The way the arch of its neon branches beckoned… in counterpoint to the rhythm to its name. The Club O-a-sis!

(short beat while she feels this rhythm)

You don't expect to happen on such a thing. Not in New York City. A pool holding out such promise for the lost and the weary.

BAR MAN. This pool's about to close. I have an appointment.

ZELDA. *(checking her watch)* At three in the morning?

(BAR MAN wipes piano top down.)

BAR MAN. With the amazing "Mrs. D."

ZELDA. At her supper club?

(She crosses back to the bar and sits.)

What's that barracuda want with the likes of you?

*(turns on stool and looks at **BAR MAN**)*

Never mind. I can figure that out. You're strong. Well put together...

BAR MAN. Wrong, Darlin'. This appointment's strictly business. Mrs. D. doesn't want this body, she wants my songs.

ZELDA. You're a musician?

BAR MAN. Sure am. I write tunes, too. And if Mrs. D. can help get those songs of mine noticed...

ZELDA. But under whose name?

BAR MAN. All I know is she showed up last week, and stayed through both sets. Said she came to hear me play. And the next thing I know, she calls. Wants to see me tonight.

ZELDA. Tonight.

BAR MAN. Me. The two bit piano man from the Oasis auditioning for a headliner like Mrs. D.

ZELDA. Just watch yourself, Sugarplum. That Great White shark thrives on well put together fry. Especially the kind with perfect, you know, pitch.

BAR MAN. I can take care of myself.

ZELDA. Just remember tomorrow, I warned you about her tonight.

(a beat)

BAR MAN. Almost done?

ZELDA. Do you want me to go?

BAR MAN. Would be nice.

ZELDA. Then so I shall! Just as soon as I finish this very hot, head-clearing coffee. This java-jive which you've kindly set before me.

(She fans the cup with her hand.)

BAR MAN. Want some ice to cool it down?

ZELDA. Oh, where's your problem, Sugar? Her final set at "The Club Delight" never wraps up until four. You show up too soon and you'll just have to twiddle your thumbs.

(**BAR MAN** *looks at his watch.*)

So, unless that's how you *want* to appear…as a "twiddler"? I'd say you've got at least an hour to kill. Lots of time for this coffee to cool and for me to… figure.

(*Realizing that he does have time to spare,* **BAR MAN** *sits at the piano. He plays. He fools with a bass line and chord combination…then he modifies it, clearly working out a tune of his own creation.*)

Nice progression, Piano Man.

BAR MAN. I do club dates in the Boroughs. And every Monday I'm here from eight until close.

(*He continues to play.*)

ZELDA. Damn. You are good!

(**BAR MAN** *realizes he has an appreciative audience. His playing becomes more enthusiastic as he swings into a full jazz arrangement. He really gets into his music.*)

Good talent makes me jealous. Mean and green.

BAR MAN. I'm still mixing drinks for a living.

ZELDA. But in a *piano* bar, Sugarplum. A place to develop your talent.

BAR MAN. This isn't Carnegie Hall.

ZELDA. That's the stage to which you aspire?

BAR MAN. Once upon a time.

ZELDA. And now?

(**BAR MAN** *closes the piano lid.*)

BAR MAN. Mrs. D. has a Steinway. She says she'll let me use it for inspiration.

ZELDA. You couldn't just rent a piano? It would be cleaner.

BAR MAN. Can't afford it. Besides… My pad's too small to fit an accordion in.

ZELDA. Then I sympathize, Jelly Bean. Unrequited passion is always a thankless itch.

BAR MAN. Yes, Ma'am.

ZELDA. Don't you dare to call me "Ma'am"! Call me Sweetheart like everyone else. Or Minnie Mouse.

BAR MAN. Minnie Mouse?

ZELDA. My reflection in this cup, upside down and backwards. The one watching me, watching you…you little toddler!

BAR MAN. Hey, I'm no kid.

ZELDA. Well, from this far side of thirty…uh, oh. Oops.

(a beat)

If you *ever* let on I admitted to such an age…

BAR MAN. You'll do what?

ZELDA. I don't know but it will be memorable.

(She bats her eyelashes. He laughs.)

*(**BAR MAN** finds a hat which has been left behind by a patron. It is a straw boater, which **BAR MAN** tries on. He considers his appearance in the bar mirror, then starts to toss it into the Lost and Found Box.)*

I gave my husband a hat like that once for fun.

*(**BAR MAN** puts the hat back on his head and transforms into **SCOTT**.)*

SCOTT. What a swell gift, Baby!

ZELDA. So glad you like it, Scott.

SCOTT. I adore it, Light of my Life.

*(**SCOTT** takes **ZELDA**'s hand and kisses it.)*

ZELDA. Oh, Goofo! You always say just the sweetest things.

SCOTT. My multi-talented prism of pulchritude.

ZELDA. Multi-talented?

SCOTT. You write, don't you? And paint, and dance?

ZELDA. Why so I do! But my talent doesn't soar in the same way yours does.

SCOTT. You haven't worked at soaring as long as I have. But stick with it Minnie, and someday? Your talent will take off like mine!

ZELDA. You promise?

SCOTT. How can it not with my help and with my love!

ZELDA. Oh, Goofo! You've no idea how much this means to me!

(**SCOTT** *reaches for her hand. He kisses it, then promenades her back to the bar, where he twirls her back onto her barstool.*)

Well, if you aren't just the most extraordinary…

(**SCOTT** *takes off the hat, and transforms back to* **BAR MAN**. *He tosses the hat into the Lost and Found box and continues to clean.*)

Oh, dear. Oh dear me. For a second I thought you were…

BAR MAN. Who?

ZELDA. Never mind. I was mistaken.

BAR MAN. You're lucky is all I can say.

ZELDA. I am? How so?

BAR MAN. You have Scott Fitzgerald's star shining in your corner.

ZELDA. The effect of "star shine," like moon shine, is often a headache.

BAR MAN. There have to be benefits, too.

ZELDA. Small consolations.

BAR MAN. You don't get noticed from having your name linked with his?

ZELDA. Noticed? Hell! Every time someone opens his novels, I get noticed. I *am* those novels, Sugar. Scott's real-life myth-in-process! Only aspire to something unique of my own design? I get written out, and of my own damned story!

BAR MAN. You don't get to claim what's yours?

ZELDA. I am only allowed to be Scott Fitzgerald's muse. His companion and sometimes "stand-in."

BAR MAN. Sounds rough.

ZELDA. I'm so tired of being someone else's fiction!

(She covers her mouth, then her eyes with her hands. She is clearly distraught.)

(BAR MAN picks up small notepad which has been left on the bar and transforms into REPORTER. He raps on the bar as he takes a business card from his pocket.)

REPORTER. Excuse me? Is anyone home? I, uh, called earlier. From the Sunday supplement?

ZELDA. Oh, yes. Yes, of course.

(ZELDA regains her composure as REPORTER enters the scene.)

(She stands. They shake hands.)

REPORTER. What a pleasure this is. To be granted an interview with F. Scott Fitzgerald!

ZELDA. Why, yes. It is, isn't it? Only Scott's not home.

REPORTER. When I phoned, you assured me that he would be back by two.

ZELDA. I did say that, didn't I?

(She flashes her smile at him.)

Looks like I was wrong. Not to worry though, Mr. Reporter-Man. Scott may not be here but *I* can give you a story.

REPORTER. On his latest novel?

ZELDA. If not on that, on what's equally compelling.

REPORTER. Well, golly gee. Fan-tastic!

(He takes in the room.)

So this is where the wonder boy does his writing.

ZELDA. And the same holds true for me.

REPORTER. And that desk. That's where the great Fitzgerald sits?

ZELDA. That's where *I* sit when I'm drafting out *my* stories.

REPORTER. I didn't realize…

ZELDA. …that I write, too? Oh, my yes! I author short stories. Quite good ones, actually.

REPORTER. I'm sure they are. I am sure they're the cat's meow! So. If you sit in *this* chair, your husband sits where? Mrs. Fitzgerald?

ZELDA. Wherever the spirit moves. But usually there. In the corner.

REPORTER. Just as I imagined. A work space sleek, yet organized. With everything so perfectly…perfectly… what?

ZELDA. Accessible?

REPORTER. Precisely the word I was after.

ZELDA. My pleasure to supply it.

REPORTER. And just look at all of these pencils! But why no typewriter, Mrs. Fitzgerald?

ZELDA. We both write our drafts in longhand.

REPORTER. Interesting.

ZELDA. In pencil, for Scott. Always. As for me? I use Crayola, whenever I'm feeling vibrant!

REPORTER. Perhaps you could give me more background.

ZELDA. Background?

REPORTER. Exactly. From the distaff point of view.

ZELDA. How do you mean?

REPORTER. Wifely anecdotes?

ZELDA. You want anecdotes.

REPORTER. Such a hit with our readership.

ZELDA. Anecdotes.

REPORTER. If you have some to spare.

(*From the bar,* **ZELDA** *gets out a bottle.*)

ZELDA. I couldn't interest you in something with more of a kick?

REPORTER. Johnny Walker! Golly gee! And despite Prohibition!

ZELDA. Like the fourth estate, our estate still has its sources.

(She offers him a drink.)

I also write literary reviews. Many of which have been published. Many times.

(She walks back to the bar for some cigarettes in a manner that is both sexy and self-assured. **REPORTER** *grows uncomfortable.)*

REPORTER. I should come back another time. When things may be more convenient.

ZELDA. Things aren't convenient now?

(She flashes him a million-dollar smile and offers a cigarette. **REPORTER** *refuses.)*

The writing I'm proudest of was for College Humor. That's a nationally distributed...

*(***REPORTER*** *looks at his watch.)*

REPORTER. How, uh, long do you think, before your husband returns?

ZELDA. I haven't the foggiest notion.

(She smiles again.)

I was thinking a *short* article about my own work...

REPORTER. This is all very kind, but...

ZELDA. Hey! I'm giving an interview, aren't I! That doesn't count for something?

REPORTER. I should come back another time. When the three of us can chat.

(He drains his glass.)

Yes, that would be better. Much better. You'll tell your Hubby?

*(***REPORTER*** *hands her a business card, then turns on his heels and leaves.)*

*(***ZELDA*** *is shocked and angered.)*

ZELDA. College Humor not good enough for you? Well, tough toenails, you two-bit stringer. Burn in Hell!

(She goes back to the bar with **REPORTER**'s *business card, which she starts to ignite, using a lighter which she takes from her purse.)*

*(***REPORTER*** has transformed into* **BAR MAN**. *He notices* **ZELDA** *with the lit lighter.)*

BAR MAN. Hey! No roasting yourself. Not on my watch!

ZELDA. A naughty habit of mine...playing with fire.

BAR MAN. And you're proud of this?

ZELDA. What artist worthy of note doesn't do the same?

*(***BAR MAN*** finds a cigar in an ashtray, which he inspects.)*

Scott encourages me to push buttons and envelopes too. So that he can record my antics and file them away.

BAR MAN. Like being escorted from hotels by the house detective?

ZELDA. So you do know me from the tabloids!

BAR MAN. Or receiving guests while you're bathing in the tub?

ZELDA. The more outrageous I am the more Scott likes it. I think it's because I'm not afraid to "act out."

BAR MAN. And he is?

ZELDA. Most times. Has to do with how he was raised. And so long as I take the lead, it's all fun and games. But let Hemingway horn in...

(She starts to itch.)

*(***BAR MAN*** transforms into* **ERNEST HEMINGWAY** *with his cigar.)*

ERNEST HEMINGWAY. Hey, Golden Girl! Where's your monkey's uncle hiding?

ZELDA. He's in seclusion, Ernest.

ERNEST HEMINGWAY. Not a problem. He'll see me.

ZELDA. He'll not! He's working! I've the strictest orders he's not to be disturbed.

ERNEST HEMINGWAY. Your lover-boy and I have a rendezvous.

ZELDA. You're admitting that? To my face? To a rendezvous!

ERNEST HEMINGWAY. An appointment, Love. Get with the language.

ZELDA. English isn't your mother tongue, the same as mine is?

ERNEST HEMINGWAY. When on the Riviera, do as the French.

ZELDA. I'm sure you do. I just wish you wouldn't do it, with my husband.

ERNEST HEMINGWAY. I commend your imagination, Honey-Curls. You should try your hand at writing.

ZELDA. I'm working on it, Slug. As I trust you're working to master the complex sentence.

ERNEST HEMINGWAY. Scott, Honey, Marseilles awaits!

(**ERNEST HEMINGWAY** *swishes toward the bedroom in a way intended to rile* **ZELDA**. *She is horrified. He stops and laughs uproariously.*)

Good God! You are such a twit!

(*She screams, as she grabs peanuts off of the bar and throws them after him.*)

ZELDA. Aaagh!

(**HEMINGWAY** *transforms into* **BAR MAN**.)

BAR MAN. Now you're *really* being more trouble than you're worth!

(**BAR MAN** *gets out a broom and dustpan, and cleans up the peanuts.*)

ZELDA. I'm sorry.

(*genuinely upset*)

So, *so* sorry. It's just…

BAR MAN. Are you going to cry? Please tell me you won't do that.

ZELDA. I don't do tears, Jelly Bean. Tears make you rust. And when you're a dancer, as am I, you need to stay mobile.

(**ZELDA** *forces herself off the bar stool and into a dance. This is an attempt to feel better about herself...more in control.*)

(*to the tune of "**BY THE SEA**" [1914] in public domain*)

BY THE SEA, FANCY FREE, COME GET NAKED WITH ME. SWILLING GIN, IN THE SWIM, UNAMBIGUOUSLY!

(*a beat*)

What's the matter? You don't like my lyrics?

BAR MAN. I would like you to finish up.

(**ZELDA** *gets a napkin from the bar, and wipes her brow as she calms herself. She regards the napkin she has been holding.*)

ZELDA. I couldn't agree with you more. Finishing up is what... Oh my!

(*She regards the napkin stack.*)

You haven't got scissors have you, Sugar Plum?

BAR MAN. No. Why?

(*She tears at a napkin fashioning a creation. Paper bits fall onto the floor.*)

Hey!

ZELDA. What? A true artist doesn't move when the spirit moves them?

BAR MAN. Well, yeah...but within limits.

ZELDA. The trick, of course, is to keep yourself in control.

(*She turns another napkin into a rose.*)

Outside, you can't always do that...go for broke. Might scare people off and then they won't give you your chance.

BAR MAN. For what?

ZELDA. For being recognized, of course. And worthy of your single perfect rose. The one bestowed on talent appreciated.

*(Although she remains seated, **ZELDA** acknowledges an imaginary audience with body language suggestive of a ballerina taking a bow...one hand to her heart showing love and appreciation. She gives the rose to the **BAR MAN**.)*

BAR MAN. A paper rose?

ZELDA. After a fashion.

BAR MAN. I didn't know paper napkins qualified as art.

ZELDA. Everything qualifies Sugar, when it comes from here...

(She points to her heart.)

...and if it transforms someone else in the teeniest way.

BAR MAN. OK, I guess. If you say so.

*(As **ZELDA** fashions the next cut-out, she sings the beginning of the children's song, "**LES PETITES MARIONETTES**.")*

ZELDA.

AINSI FONT FONT FONT, LES PETITES MARIONNETTES.
AINSI FONT, FONT, FONT, TROIS PETITES TOURS ET PUIS S'EN VONT.

(a beat)

Before I used to make simple representations. Paper dolls of Scott, and of me, and of our little girl, Scottie. Only recently, my fingers seem to take off. On their own. And before I realize, there's paper doll Goldilocks, and Rumpelstiltskin...and the entire court of Louis the Fourteenth, lined up. All set to promenade our living room floor!

BAR MAN. Sounds like a lot of work...

ZELDA. Not work, Sugarplum. Magic.

(a beat)

ZELDA. A pity you've got no scissors. Flights of fancy take off ever so much better when you have the proper...

BAR MAN. Tools?

ZELDA. The proper runway. To launch vision after ever more glorious vision!

(She tosses paper scraps up into the air. She bats at them with her hands to keep them from falling.)

BAR MAN. Hey! Watch the confetti!

ZELDA. Oh, for heavens sake! I'll clean up, once I'm done.

*(**BAR MAN** hands her the dustpan and whisk broom.)*

BAR MAN. You'll clean as you go. Or we'll both clean up paper all night!

*(**BAR MAN** gets a wastebasket from behind the bar and sets it before her. **ZELDA** puts her paper scraps into it.)*

ZELDA. Oh, diddle pooh! You're no fun at all! How am I to release a true artistic passion, when all I'm allowed is to keep things neat and tidy.

BAR MAN. That wasn't how I meant.

ZELDA. How did you mean it then? And don't give me Scott's old saw: "How every page needs a margin... every canvas, an edge..."

*(**BAR MAN** returns to what he was doing, then transforms into **SCOTT**.)*

SCOTT. ...Every tune needs a staff to hold the notes squarely in place.

ZELDA. But why, Dearest Heart? And not because "you said so."

SCOTT. The true artist knows how to frame.

ZELDA. Only sometimes, edges confine. Mama used to be "pure music," until we framed her. Drew her borders too tight. Wound up choking off her spirit.

SCOTT. You're not your mother. You're Zelda. The most extraordinary woman in this world! And if you develop the discipline you're lacking? Then "watch out," world, is all I have to say!

ZELDA. So, all my work needs to get noticed is discipline? Hell, I can do that. Do that all the time for Madame Egorova.

(She turns playful.)

And, surely if I can show such discipline in her dance class, then I can apply the same rigor to my writing... without risking, rigor mortis!

*(****SCOTT*** *laughs and gives her a peck. He exits the stage.)*

No, wait! Don't go.

SCOTT. I have to work.

ZELDA. But without you beside me encouraging, I'll implode!

*(****ZELDA*** *reaches towards him but is brought back into the "reality" of the bar by the itching of her eczema. She scratches at her arm. A beat. She slaps at her hand.)*

You stop this, Minnie Mouse! You stop your scratching...unless you want doctors to trundle out their bandages...or worse.

(She tries to restrain her hands.)

Except I itch!

(She wants to scratch her arm but fights the impulse.)

Maybe if I practice.

(She stands, placing her still folded up cutout creation on the bar. She takes hold of the railing of the bar, relating to it as though it were a ballet barre. She does some simple plies as she sings.)

AINSI FONT FONT FONT, LES PETITES MARIONNETTES.
AINSI FONT FONT FONT, TROIS PETITES TOURS ET PUIS S'EN
    VONT.

*(****ZELDA*** *performs a simple turn successfully. Emboldened, she attempts something more complex...ending with a*

fouette turn…which she cannot do without losing her balance. She grabs the bar rail for stability.)

Curses, Minnie! Foiled again! Failed. Foiled. Failed.

(ZELDA *hangs onto the bar rail, defeated.)*

(BAR MAN *returns to the stage as* **MME. EGOROVA,** **ZELDA***'s ballet teacher.)*

MME. EGOROVA. So early for practice today?

ZELDA. Madame Egorova?

MME. EGOROVA. My studio door is open for you, Daragousha. *(translation: "Dear One")*

ZELDA. I'm not here to dance today.

MME. EGOROVA. You are not feeling good?

ZELDA. I feel lousy.

MME. EGOROVA. Is change in the weather, perhaps. These winters here in Paris, so grey. So heartless. We dancers are knowing this. In the bones! In the teeth!

ZELDA. It's not the weather, Madame. I'm just sick at heart.

MME. EGOROVA. Heavy heart, for Artist, is usual condition. For *Russian* artist, that is.

ZELDA. I don't really know how to say this to you…

MME. EGOROVA. Not to talk, then. To talk is something for cynics. And revolutionaries. By movement is how we dancers must be expressing. By beautiful line, and with most exquisite grace.

(MME. EGOROVA *taps out a rhythm with her cane.)*

And one two three, and one two three.

(ZELDA *straightens up as if about to embark on a dance movement. She checks her body posture and her alignment as she prepares. She is totally focused.)*

(She moves into a first position stance, arms down and relaxed. She takes a breath and begins.)

ZELDA. The San Carlo Opera Ballet Company. My debut, Madame?

(MME. EGOROVA *continues to tap out a solid rhythm.)*

MME. EGOROVA. And one two three...

ZELDA. *(The words tumble out.)* I can't accept their offer or their contract.

(**MME. EGOROVA** *stops tapping.*)

MME. EGOROVA. Not to accept? When professional recognition is all we work for?

ZELDA. I'm sorry. It's just...I'm married.

MME. EGOROVA. As are many. But many are not beginning career at old age of twenty seven.

ZELDA. I know that, Madame.

MME. EGOROVA. Then continue, Zelda. One, two, three... One, two...

(**ZELDA** *doesn't move.*)

ZELDA. I also know how in Europe, people think differently. So different from the way people think back home.

MME. EGOROVA. Be happy then you've aligned yourself with our people. Where "The Rite of Spring" is revered, not considered obscene.

ZELDA. When you grow up as I did in Alabama? When it comes to certain things? You do what's expected.

MME. EGOROVA. For three and a half years, you come to my studio. You practice, more than any other student. You make progress. Much progress and so, despite your age, I write letters. Many letters for you, Daragousha. To friends. To compatriots. And now that opportunity is being given, you can not see clear for this chance to be embracing?

ZELDA. Scott's father is sick. We have to go to be with him. We have to be by his side...in *Minnesota*.

MME. EGOROVA. Minnesota?

ZELDA. I can't debut in *Gisele*.

(**ZELDA** *starts to cry.*)

MME. EGOROVA. My poor, poor Daragousha! For so many years you struggle for this recognition!

(ZELDA goes to MME. EGOROVA's outstretched arms. MME. EGOROVA embraces ZELDA.)

So much feet are blistering. Toes bleeding! And always, with a smile and determination. And such fortitude…

ZELDA. My husband…my family needs me. I have to do what's expected.

MME. EGOROVA. If this is true then my time you are wasting, Zelda. My time, and your money.

(Her feelings are deeply hurt.)

All wasted.

ZELDA. I have no choice!

(MME. EGOROVA exits. A beat.)

Damned strings! Always sticking, engulfing, entangling me like cobwebs!

(ZELDA brushes imaginary strings away from her arms.)

BAR MAN. Not sure what you're doing, but stop it.

(Exhausted, ZELDA puts her head down on folded arms. BAR MAN notices ZELDA's folded cutout, which he unfolds. It's a chain of musical notes.)

Hey! Pretty nifty!

ZELDA. You think?

BAR MAN. Very original.

ZELDA. It's for you, then. A gift. As one artist to another.

(The BAR MAN is touched by her gesture.)

BAR MAN. What note would you say that this is?

ZELDA. Looks like a "G" to me. Yeah. Definitely.

BAR MAN. I could have used this last week-end at that wedding. The father of the bride kept requesting this melody.

ZELDA. Which one?

BAR MAN. You'll know the tune.

(He crosses back to the piano and plays.)

ZELDA. "The Minuet in G"?

BAR MAN. Problem was the piano in the reception hall had a slow key. The kind that takes forever to come back up?

ZELDA. Not the G!

BAR MAN. Bingo!

(ZELDA giggles.)

ZELDA. How to play that tune when you're missing the main attraction?

BAR MAN. You transpose it up a half step and then you wing it!

ZELDA. And no one caught on? I love it!

BAR MAN. They could have cared less.

ZELDA. You cared.

BAR MAN. How I was trained.

(She looks at him quizzically.)

At Peabody?

ZELDA. You studied there? I'm impressed.

BAR MAN. Don't be. I didn't graduate. I, uh, can't read music.

ZELDA. Big deal.

BAR MAN. It was for them.

ZELDA. If that's true, then why would they let you into their program?

BAR MAN. I have this really great ear. Only, once they found out I was faking, they dropped me. Flat.

ZELDA. Ouch.

BAR MAN. And me supposed to be Rachmaninoff's heir.

ZELDA. But if you couldn't read music...

BAR MAN. I could play just like the best of them! I memorized records. Every single disc Rachmaninoff ever recorded. Every record made by those other Maestros, too. Hofmann. Hesse. Moisewitsch... I've got all of their moves memorized...for technique and for style.

ZELDA. You couldn't just have learned to read your notes? Once you saw how such a thing could be important?

BAR MAN. I look at a page, and those little black dots seem to slide...

ZELDA. ...between *their* staff and *your* brain.

(*ZELDA understands.*)

BAR MAN. How'd you know?

ZELDA. A lot that makes no sense to most...makes perfect sense to me.

(*a beat*)

BAR MAN. The sight reading final did me in.

ZELDA. Even though you could prove that, once you hear something, you can play it?

BAR MAN. Note for note.

ZELDA. Then, you got skunked, and that stinks.

BAR MAN. Hey, it's over, and it's O.K. I got in my licks.

(*confiding*)

I transposed myself. Started fooling around with what suited me better. Jazz.

(*He plays an up-tempo riff.*)

ZELDA. Where the only notes someone gives a damn for are the ones written down in your head!

(*She claps her hands, delighted.*)

Oh, good! A happy ending! I like happy endings! Had one myself, once upon a time you know. One of my more positive "inside" moments. Why the whole draft for my novel just came gushing forth. It was like the words were already written down inside of my head. And all I had to do was...

BAR MAN. ...copy them out!

(*They have made a connection.*)

ZELDA. *Save Me the Waltz?*

BAR MAN. I'd love to but like I said… I've got plans later on.

ZELDA. No, silly! That's the name of my book! The one that got published.

BAR MAN. Really?

ZELDA. And not by some vanity press!

BAR MAN. Well, congratulations!

ZELDA. Thank you. It really *was* quite wonderful. Even though I was still on the "inside," I was so "out there!" And the most remarkable part? It only took three months to get the draft done. Not three, or four or five *years*, like *some* people I know.

(She puts her head down on the bar. **BAR MAN** *transforms into* **SCOTT**.*)*

SCOTT. While you were off recuperating, Zelda…

ZELDA. Not now, please, Scott. Not Now.

SCOTT. I got a letter. From Max.

ZELDA. *(worried)* At Scribner's?

SCOTT. What other Max do we know?

ZELDA. How is the dear boy?

SCOTT. You sent him a completed manuscript.

*(***SCOTT*** *gets out a bottle.)*

ZELDA. Just a draft for an opinion.

SCOTT. When you know you're to get mine first?

ZELDA. But I *did* send you a copy. Months ago. Which you've yet to acknowledge.

SCOTT. You had no right to send my editor anything!

ZELDA. Hey, it's not as if I didn't want your critique!

(controlling herself)

Darling Heart, I sent Max my draft, so I'd have *two* opinions to work from. Two critiques for when I start my revisions.

SCOTT. You did this for spite.

ZELDA. I did not!

SCOTT. For years you've been reading *my* manuscript to *my* novel. Probably memorized whole sections.

(He pours another shot and drinks it to spite her.)

ZELDA. *(uncomprehending)* This is all because Max wants to publish me?

SCOTT. *(controlling his rage)* For years, now, I've sidetracked my energy from my *real* work to finance your medical bills.

ZELDA. Did I ask to be kept in a *private* sanitarium?

SCOTT. I won't have you cared for in anyplace less than the best.

ZELDA. And I appreciate that.

SCOTT. Even though it means writing crap. Three thousand turd magazine pieces to make ends meet!

ZELDA. Why must you always think of me as some hopeless drudge?

SCOTT. You are purposely ruining me.

ZELDA. Please don't spoil my homecoming, Scott.

SCOTT. Me? The spoiler?

ZELDA. I'm going to be published. Be happy for me!

*(**SCOTT** pours yet another shot.)*

Oh, this is intolerable. All the while I was inside and free to be expansive…the most creative soul in the whole damn galaxy…I kept saying "no." This isn't how things should be. I don't want us to be estranged.

(a beat)

Only now that I'm outside again? Oh, Goofo. This isn't the marriage that either one of us wants.

SCOTT. It's the one we're stuck with.

ZELDA. Well, I can't stay stuck with it longer! I want a divorce.

SCOTT. You can't have one. My family's Catholic.

ZELDA. Please, Scott. I can't go back to the way things were. I can't keep painting maps on the garden furniture!

(**SCOTT** *stares at his glass. He turns his back and exits.*)

No, wait! Dearest, don't turn your back on me! You do, and I break out in hives. All along my neck...my mouth...

(She gets a mirror and lipstick from her pocketbook. She examines her face.)

Dear God.

(**SCOTT** *returns to the stage as the* **BAR MAN**.)

BAR MAN. What now?

ZELDA. This face, Jelly Bean. Like stale smoke, when it should look like...this!

(Using her lipstick, she draws an outline of "lips" on the table top.)

BAR MAN. What the Hell?

ZELDA. My lips. My portrait close up.

(puckering her lips in a kiss)

You can't see the resemblance?

BAR MAN. You are nuts.

ZELDA. What original isn't!

BAR MAN. Your purse.

ZELDA. What for?

BAR MAN. A phone number. I'm calling your husband.

ZELDA. Can't we leave Scott out of this? Please?

BAR MAN. Your pocketbook, Mrs. Fitzgerald.

(She gives it to him.)

ZELDA. My husband isn't home. He's never at home. Not until the party's over and he's off to God knows where. With all of those flirts and society matrons who hang on his every word...

BAR MAN. And you've just come from such a party.

(**ZELDA** *begins to sing* **"THE ABA DABA HONEYMOON"** *[in public domain, copyright 1914] as, with her finger, she re-traces her lips on the table.)*

ZELDA.

> ABA DABA DABA DABA DABA DABA DABA
> SAID THE MONKEY TO THE CHIMP.
> ABA DABA DABA DABA DABA DABA DABA
> SAID THE CHIMPIE TO THE MONK.

(She starts to Charleston.)

> ALL DAY LONG, THEY CHATTED AWAY.
> ALL NIGHT LONG, THEY WERE HAPPY AND GAY.
> SINGING AND SWINGING IN A HONKY-TONKY...

*(**ZELDA** stops her dance in mid-kick. She deflates.)*

BAR MAN. Seriously, Sweetheart, who *can* I call?

ZELDA. I haven't the foggiest.

BAR MAN. A relative? Friend? Family doctor?

ZELDA. No doctors. No.

BAR MAN. You've got a better solution?

ZELDA. What I'm trying to come up with, Jelly Bean. A solution for myself. Only nothing's forthcoming.

(In frustration, she upends a bar stool. It falls over onto the floor.)

(Both take in what she has done.)

*(**BAR MAN** sets the stool back on its legs. He goes behind the bar and gets a phone out. He sets this phone on the bar.)*

BAR MAN. The cops, then. To see you home safely.

(He starts to dial. She pushes the disconnect button.)

ZELDA. When I get in my moods, I know I do putrid things. All of which I regret most desperately later on. But if "turning me in" is that thing that has to happen? Can't you leave me to do that insult to myself? For myself if that's how I decide?

BAR MAN. Move your finger. Please.

ZELDA. I'll make trouble.

BAR MAN. You already have.

ZELDA. *(switching gears into a teasing mode)* I'll make more. Do you want to wind up in the tabloids?

BAR MAN. Get out.

ZELDA. Oh, diddle pooh! Can't you tell when a girl's just having some fun? All right. You win. Once I clean up my act...

(She starts to wipe the "lips" from off the tabletop.)

BAR MAN. Then you'll go?

ZELDA. Once I can see my way clear to a happy ending. Pretty please with sugar on it? Be a peach?

(She goes back to cleaning the lipstick with a vengeance. **BAR MAN** *puts the phone away under the bar.)*

But can I ever really divorce my one and only? When my Darling and I have been joined at the hip for so long?

*(***BAR MAN*** *transforms into* **SCOTT***.)*

SCOTT. At the heart, too, Baby. We're joined at the hip *and* the heart.

ZELDA. Of course, Scott, Dearest. Two souls, created as one. Joined, forever and ever. And ever, and ever and...

*(***ZELDA*** *turns away from* **SCOTT** *as she slides into a depression.)*

*(***SCOTT*** *is oblivious to her mood swing.)*

SCOTT. God alone knows why I find you so enchanting.

ZELDA. *(fighting to pull herself out of the depression)* I need you to embellish on that motif!

SCOTT. You need me to elaborate?

ZELDA. *(with a weak laugh)* If I don't know how you think of me truly, then how am I to know what to think of myself?

SCOTT. All right. I'll confide. You're perfect.

(He goes to her. They nuzzle.)

ZELDA. You don't think that at all! You think that I'm as lazy as a blowfish!

SCOTT. But such a charming blowfish!

ZELDA. The truth, Dearest Heart. Do you really, *really* love me?

SCOTT. Desperately.

ZELDA. Why?

SCOTT. Because you're charming.

ZELDA. You've said that. Another reason.

SCOTT. Because you'll listen to all of my manuscripts? Daytime, night time, Saturdays, too!

ZELDA. Keep going.

SCOTT. Because you clean out the icebox! At least once a week!

(She throws her arms around him playfully.)

ZELDA. You do love your Minnie Mouse! And for more reasons than just the pleasure giving ones!

(She kisses him.)

SCOTT. My moon! My muse! My Salome!

(Another kiss, this time initiated by **SCOTT**. *She returns the kiss passionately. A beat.)*

ZELDA. Scott, stop. We have to get changed.

SCOTT. We're going out? Again?

ZELDA. We have tickets for George White's new *Scandals*.

SCOTT. I had planned on writing.

ZELDA. *(heartbroken)* Oh, Darling Heart!

SCOTT. Can't help it, Minnie. Your Goofo has a deadline.

ZELDA. You *always* have deadlines. Excuses however lame.

*(***SCOTT*** turns out of the scene, and transforms into the* **BAR MAN**. *He rolls up his sleeves and begins to put chairs on the tables.* **ZELDA** *notices his physique.)*

What a simply extraordinary shirt, Jelly Bean. Great color.

BAR MAN. It's white.

ZELDA. The color of starch. You remind me of a Frenchman I once knew.

*(A beat as **ZELDA** pulls herself back from the brink of yet another threatening downward slide. She re-composes herself, by vamping the **BAR MAN**.)*

So, Sport! Want to go away together? Want to lie side by side on some strand and get berry brown?

BAR MAN. You don't really mean that. Do you?

ZELDA. No, but such a fabulous thought! So well turned out. So gloriously extended. I should write that down.

(She gets out a pencil and a journal from her pocketbook and starts to write. She stops.)

Ah, why bother. I'll never get any credit. Even though I pen the words in my very own hand.

(She leaves the book open faced down and turns away.)

*(**BAR MAN** moves to look at **ZELDA**'s journal. She sees and stops him.)*

Hey! Just like all of the others aren't you! No respect at all for my personal property.

BAR MAN. I thought, since you left it open…

ZELDA. I left it faced down.

BAR MAN. I'm sorry.

(He hangs his head.)

Really sorry.

(She closes the book and holds it.)

So what is it, anyway? A diary?

(She turns the book in her hands.)

ZELDA. More like a journal and sketch pad all rolled in one. Ah, go ahead. You can look.

(She puts her book back on the bar.)

BAR MAN. Really?

ZELDA. You apologized, didn't you?

BAR MAN. You're sure?

(She doesn't answer. A beat.)

ZELDA. My instincts tell me that we are kindred spirits.

(He opens the book hesitantly and looks inside.)

Scott encourages me to work. To fill up pages. Keeps me off his back while he's traipsing around without me.

BAR MAN. These words. This style. It's the same as you read in *Gatsby*.

ZELDA. It is, isn't it?

(A beat, as the **BAR MAN** *continues to flip through the book.)*

BAR MAN. All these sketches, too.

ZELDA. I have many gifts.

BAR MAN. I can see that.

(He continues to flip through the pages.)

ZELDA. Scott dallies, you know. From here to the Riviera. With every rouged knee and rolled down stocking that will let him.

BAR MAN. You don't dally, yourself?

ZELDA. I flirt.

BAR MAN. Your distinction escapes me.

ZELDA. It's one thing to let the public enjoy me as a "flapper." But when it comes to my private parts? Those, I keep to myself. As should you...with Mrs. D.

BAR MAN. Not really your business. Besides...it's not like I'm married.

ZELDA. Not even to your music?

BAR MAN. Well sure, I'm wed to that.

ZELDA. Then don't go selling it out to some jive talkin' Mama.

BAR MAN. Mrs. D. isn't jiving with me. She loves my songs and...

ZELDA. And what?

BAR MAN. She, uh, wants me to be her accompanist. Build a whole new act for herself around my music.

ZELDA. In exchange for what?

BAR MAN. I'll get more specifics tonight.

ZELDA. Are you really that desperate, Sugar?

(BAR MAN *resumes his stacking up the chairs.*)

That you're willing to sell your soul to be kept on a leash?

BAR MAN. No one keeps me.

ZELDA. She will.

(*short beat*)

Listen up, Sugar Plum. You've the curse of the gifted few. It's what makes you so susceptible to people like her.

BAR MAN. You know nothing about me.

ZELDA. I know how you play. You have demons. I hear them locked up inside of your every chord.

BAR MAN. What are you talking about?

ZELDA. Relax. A demon can be a good thing. A demon's what makes good work so...well, so compelling.

BAR MAN. So this is a compliment?

ZELDA. No. It's a vote of confidence, Sugar. Only unlike Mrs. D.'s this one comes without strings.

(ZELDA *motions for the* BAR MAN *to give back her journal. He does.*)

True artists have strings enough. They tie us down while others keep tripping us up and pulling our focus away from what's important.

BAR MAN. And what would that be?

ZELDA. The work of course. All the work that needs to get out there and be recognized.

(ZELDA *goes back to writing and sketching.* BAR MAN *continues his cleaning.* ZELDA *puts down her pen. She offers her journal in the direction of the* BAR MAN.)

Scott? Darling-Heart?

(**BAR MAN** *transforms into* **SCOTT**.)

SCOTT. Yes, Minnie Mouse?

(*She offers her journal again. He doesn't take it.*)

What's this?

ZELDA. My piece for the magazine. It's as done as I can get it.

SCOTT. And you want me to…

ZELDA. Have a look. Only, this time, put your heart into it. Pretty please?

SCOTT. I don't always?

ZELDA. No.

(*short beat*)

Come on, Goofo! Please! I've been working over a month on this revision!

(*She opens the book for him. He barely looks at it.*)

SCOTT. It's the same as it was before. No sense of continuity. No sense of plot.

ZELDA. Then help me fix this thing!

SCOTT. I can't. It wouldn't be yours.

ZELDA. Who cares? Nothing that I write gets published, anyway! Not unless you approve it first and then both of our names get signed on.

SCOTT. (*defensive*) With my name attached it commands a higher price.

ZELDA. That I understand. What I *don't* get is why whole passages of my diary keep cropping up between your sheets.

SCOTT. Are you suggesting?

ZELDA. My words. Inside of your texts where they grow like weeds. Multiplying like dandelions.

SCOTT. We share the same experience is all.

ZELDA. Bull feathers. I want credit where credit is due. And I also want… I want you to teach me to realize my stories. In my own true voice like you've promised since the beginning. Either that or give me back my diary.

SCOTT. I can't.

ZELDA. Why not?

SCOTT. I loaned it out.

ZELDA. You what!

SCOTT. I loaned it.

ZELDA. You had no right...!

SCOTT. Zelda, honey, certain parts were so breathtaking I simply had to share them.

ZELDA. Breathtaking? Really? Which parts?

SCOTT. Your images, mostly. They're great. They explode, like Roman candles!

ZELDA. And what parts didn't you like?

SCOTT. Same as always. Your structure. There's no way for the reader to get from point A to point B.

ZELDA. I can't think in straight lines. Flat thinking is always so boring. And then I spend too much time with goosing things up. And that scares me, you know? That while I'm off making adjustments...life's passing me by.

SCOTT. Life's hardly passing you by, my one and only! Not when our duo's about to become a trio!

(ZELDA *regards her belly self-consciously.*)

ZELDA. You had to remind me.

SCOTT. That my Minnie Mouse is bearing my heir apparent?

ZELDA. Minnie Mouse doesn't have children.

SCOTT. Well, *my* Minnie does! My Minnie Mouse breaks new ground!

ZELDA. This is happening way too fast! I don't know that I'm ready to be so confined.

SCOTT. Confinement's a state of mind.

ZELDA. So easy to say when you're already established.

SCOTT. Look at me, Minnie Mouse. This child will be good for you. I can only imagine how giving birth would inform me artistically.

ZELDA. You? Give birth?

(**SCOTT** *releases her, embarrassed that he has revealed his own hostility towards women, who can create the kinds of things he can't. He tries to regain control of the situation in order to bolster his own self-image.*)

SCOTT. This, uh, baby of ours will be great. It will have your mouth.

ZELDA. My mouth?

SCOTT. Yes. Your dear sweet mouth!

(*He takes her face in his hands and kisses her gently on the lips. She relaxes. A playful and joking banter begins.*)

And your eyes...dark blue as midnight! And your hair, and your keister, too...but not your legs.

ZELDA. Well, he'd better not get your nose...

SCOTT. He?

ZELDA. We'd produce otherwise?

SCOTT. Possibly.

ZELDA. (*suddenly quite serious*) Dear God, I hope not. I would hate for this little one to be a girl-child.

SCOTT. Whatever we have will be wonderful, Mrs. Fitz. Because it will be ours. And because it will give you a whole new audience. For your fabulous, uh... outpourings.

ZELDA. I can see that. Yes. That's a real possibility.

(**SCOTT** *holds her another moment, then moves on.*)

Wait! Where are you going?

SCOTT. Work.

ZELDA. Not work. Not now. Not when you've got me believing how this baby might satisfy.

(**SCOTT** *transforms back into* **BAR MAN**.)

BAR MAN. Are you alright?

*(No response from **ZELDA**. He looks at his watch and then goes to the phone.)*

I have to let her know that I'll be late.

ZELDA. Mrs. D.? Don't. Please.

BAR MAN. Not your call to make.

(The line is busy. He pauses, then re-dials.)

ZELDA. If you won't listen to me, at least listen to your music.

BAR MAN. All my music needs is a place where it can be heard. By the right people and in my lifetime. Okay?

(He listens a moment, then hangs up.)

ZELDA. Line tied up? A signal, surely. A sign not to go there and tarnish your innocence.

BAR MAN. If I was that innocent, Sweetheart, I'd have my degree. Have my contracts set and be playing the concert circuit.

*(**BAR MAN** re-dials.)*

ZELDA. You still could, couldn't you? Have the career that you always wanted? Why, I'd bet, with the right kind of help, you could learn to read music. Then you could get that Conservatory credential.

*(**BAR MAN** is listening to another busy signal.)*

BAR MAN. Those Peabody bridges are burned beyond recognition.

(He slams the receiver down.)

Get off of the god-damned phone!

ZELDA. Don't be so desperate, Sugar. Desperate people do desperate things they regret later on.

(He checks his watch again.)

BAR MAN. You wouldn't understand.

*(**BAR MAN** picks up the full waste basket and exits the stage to dump it.)*

ZELDA. God damn it to Hell! No one ever wants to listen to what I say! Like how even the brightest of stars can fall from the sky, however fixed in the heavens they may appear. It's a function of the seasons. And the tide.

(BAR MAN, *having transformed into* SCOTT, *returns. He wears a Lieutenant's cap of the kind worn during the First World War.*)

SCOTT. Well, hello Jell-O! Why's a pretty girl like you standing all by her lonesome?

ZELDA. Please, Lieutenant.

SCOTT. Fitzgerald. But call me Scott.

ZELDA. Please Scott. No company now.

SCOTT. Sure, Baby. Whatever you say.

(SCOTT *pulls out a flask and takes a swig.* ZELDA *notices.*)

ZELDA. What's there?

SCOTT. Nectar from the Gods. Do you want a sip?

(*He hands her the flask. She takes a swig.*)

ZELDA. Um. Good!

SCOTT. Only the best for the best.

ZELDA. Why thank you, uh, Scott.

(*She extends her hand.*)

I'm Zelda.

SCOTT. I know that. Everyone who's anyone knows who you are, Miss Sayre.

(*A beat, as he looks at her intently.*)

ZELDA. And how long do you plan to be in little ol' Montgomery?

SCOTT. Just until Basic Training's done. Then I'll be shipped overseas. I just hope the war lasts long enough to see some real action. Kill some Krauts? Plug the Kaiser, you know? Get exotic new material for my writing.

ZELDA. Your writing?

SCOTT. My real work.

ZELDA. An author?

SCOTT. A novelist.

ZELDA. Ooh. Are you any good?

SCOTT. Damned good.

(ZELDA kisses him impulsively on the mouth.)

What was that for?

ZELDA. I like a man who knows what he's about!

SCOTT. And I like a woman who's not afraid of an impulse.

(He kisses her back.)

So, Miss Zelda Sayre, how about we have a dance? In the ballroom in front of all your society!

ZELDA. Too stuffy in there. That's why I came outside.

SCOTT. All right, then. A waltz. By the light of the silvery moon!

ZELDA. Except there's no combo playing. Not on this verandah. No music at all, to speak of.

SCOTT. We couldn't make our own?

ZELDA. I suppose we could. Why not? We can dance out here in the open. And to any damned tune that we please.

(SCOTT takes her hand and promenades her around the stage, as it were, "presenting her" to an unseen assembled.)

*(They dance an impromptu dance to "**GIRL OF MY DREAMS**," which is in the public domain.)*

(SCOTT hums/sings playfully, having a wonderful time)

(The tune gets picked up by an unseen orchestra. As they dance, the music swells. They are having a grand time together.)

SCOTT. Yowza!

(The song ends. SCOTT looks at her with great admiration.)

ZELDA. If you aren't just the most extraordinary!

SCOTT. You have more flair in your little finger...

ZELDA. In my little finger?

SCOTT. And so much élan!

ZELDA. "Élan" is good. "Élan" can be developed.

SCOTT. Up North.

ZELDA. Up North?

SCOTT. *(with a wink)* In Manhattan!

(He produces a lighter to light her a cigarette, but it only sparks. She continues on, oblivious to his problem with the lighter.)

ZELDA. Why, of course! Where Bohemian life still rules! Dominates! Pulsates!

SCOTT. Hold that thought, you irresistible confection! I need to search out a flint so we can spark!

(He exits.)

*(**ZELDA** continues to sing and to dance to "**GIRL OF MY DREAMS**." She dances alone, as before.)*

ZELDA. New York was where it all was going to happen. For me as well as for Scott.

BAR MAN. I know how it hurts when the things that you count on fall flat.

ZELDA. Why for you. Jelly Bean?

BAR MAN. I have a knack for getting it wrong, I guess.

ZELDA. Or maybe you just don't want to get it right. It's possible, isn't it? My little girl, Scottie, does wrong all the time. Why, just the other night, she was wearing nail polish! Bright red!

BAR MAN. So what?

ZELDA. At thirteen years old? Sugar Plum! Thirteen's far too young.

BAR MAN. You didn't wear polish yourself at half that age?

ZELDA. Of course, I did. But I had the sense to take it off before dinner.

BAR MAN. So maybe your kid is looking for attention.

ZELDA. Or maybe for someone to stop her, before she goes crazy.

(**BAR MAN** *transforms into* **MAMA SAYRE**. *She holds a bouquet of flowers.*)

MAMA SAYRE. Look what just got delivered, Baby-Girl.

ZELDA. How beautiful, Mama! Oh my!

(**ZELDA** *takes the flowers from* **MAMA SAYRE**. *She inhales their aroma and then examines the card.*)

And from Scott! Such a dear.

MAMA SAYRE. And where has your soldier of fortune gone off to now?

ZELDA. *(confidentially)* To Bohemia, Mama. Where all *true* artists go to get discovered.

MAMA SAYRE. I thought sure his letters were postmarked New York City.

(**ZELDA** *admires the flowers.*)

ZELDA. What's this? Something else is tucked inside here, tied to the stem.

(**ZELDA** *unties the ribbon. An engagement ring slips into her hand.*)

Oh, goodness!

(*She puts the ring on her finger.*)

MAMA SAYRE. A ring? An engagement ring?

ZELDA. Such a prism of fireworks! So pure...like our own true love!

(**MAMA SAYRE** *puts the flowers in a vase. She arranges them as she continues.*)

MAMA SAYRE. Best to add it to your collection and then forget it.

ZELDA. But this is the most promising...!

MAMA SAYRE. *(cutting her off)* Memento. That's all. From one more of your many admirers.

ZELDA. Scott's more than just an admirer, Mama. He's special.

MAMA SAYRE. Stick to your college boys, Baby. At least, we know they respect you, and mind who you are.

ZELDA. Scott respects.

MAMA SAYRE. He's a Catholic.

ZELDA. So?

MAMA SAYRE. Catholics don't believe in, let alone practice…

(She stops short.)

ZELDA. Practice what, Mama?

(a beat)

MAMA SAYRE. Just be careful, Baby, is all. We don't want our dreams for your talents to go up in smoke.

ZELDA. Scott wants me to realize my talents, the same way we do. He's given his word!

MAMA SAYRE. Well, you're making this all sound awfully serious, Baby.

ZELDA. Scott's gone to New York to get discovered, Mama. And I'm going there to join him!

MAMA SAYRE. New York? Oh, no, no, no! Not a good idea at all. You can cultivate your gifts just as well right here.

ZELDA. In Montgomery, *Alabama?* You of all people…? Mama! What about your grand adventure to Philadelphia?

MAMA SAYRE. I went there to winter with friends.

ZELDA. You were a singer, Mama!

MAMA SAYRE. A long time ago.

ZELDA. The "Wild Lily of the Cumberland."

MAMA SAYRE. Before Grandpa Machen came and yanked me home.

ZELDA. You were given a perfect rose.

MAMA SAYRE. You are mistaken.

ZELDA. A perfect rose to acknowledge a perfect talent. I've seen it in the attic, pressed in wax paper.

(a beat)

MAMA SAYRE. And you've told your young Lieutenant?

ZELDA. About what, Mama?

MAMA SAYRE. The, uh, Sayre legacy.

(*ZELDA doesn't answer.*)

For your own good, Baby. Do not keep him in the dark. Your father did that to me and I still can't forgive him!

ZELDA. I will *not* wind up like my sister...or Grandma Sayre. I'm stronger than the two of them, put together.

MAMA SAYRE. But if you're not. If you carry some kind of frailty from Daddy's side.

ZELDA. You really think their weakness is that strong?

MAMA SAYRE. Your Daddy thinks...

ZELDA. I'm not asking Daddy, Mama. I'm asking you.

MAMA SAYRE. It's always the higher spirited of Sayre women who find themselves the most susceptible. Your own sister has to go and take a "cure" every month. And poor Grandmother Sayre... Dead by her very own hand.

ZELDA. I know all this, Mama! I don't need to be reminded.

MAMA SAYRE. I worry, Baby. Should you or a girl child of yours wind up with this burden...

(*Despite her bravado,* **ZELDA**'s *confidence is shaken.*)

ZELDA. All right. All right. I'll give the matter some thought.

MAMA SAYRE. Four seasons at least.

ZELDA. I'll consider what you say.

(**ZELDA** *starts to put on the ring.*)

MAMA SAYRE. You wear that thing and the whole town will think you're engaged.

ZELDA. I thought you and Daddy want for me to marry.

MAMA SAYRE. We do. Just not him.

ZELDA. Why not? Scott's a Princeton man, and he's golden! Like the sun!

MAMA SAYRE. Daddy says he's a social climbing, ne'er do well, son of a Yankee. I say he can't hold his liquor.

(**MAMA SAYRE** *exits.* **ZELDA** *take off the ring.*)

ZELDA. All right. All right. I mean, where *is* all the rush? I can always get engaged to Scott later on. Once he's established enough to keep us both in high style. Once I've figured out how to tell of the Sayer weakness. After all I should be honest and square with the man I would marry.

(*a beat*)

Then again...such a pretty thing. And big as the Ritz!

(*She puts the ring back on, and admires it.*)

(**BAR MAN** *returns, this time with a mop and a bucket. He checks his watch and picks up the phone.*)

(**ZELDA** *takes a deep breath. A beat.*)

Mrs. D only wants to get her hands on your songs. You realize that don't you?

(*no reaction from* **BAR MAN**)

Problem is the songs she promotes are the ones she can claim. And she will claim yours for her own, make no mistake, Sugar.

BAR MAN. (*a bit too smug*) She can't do that.

ZELDA. Sure she can.

BAR MAN. How can you claim what's not written down?

ZELDA. Not written?

BAR MAN. If I can't read my notes, how to set them down on paper?

(*A beat.* **ZELDA** *grows more concerned.*)

ZELDA. And you can't get a friend? At least tell me that your songs are well protected.

(*The implication of what she's saying dawns on him.*)

BAR MAN. Can't worry about such things.

ZELDA. You'd really run the risk?

BAR MAN. I have to make my breaks and take my chances.

ZELDA. But you have your break, already. At this Oasis.

BAR MAN. And nothing's happening here!

*(**BAR MAN** storms off in frustration.)*

ZELDA. I know how it can be when you feel you're off track. I felt pretty much off track on the Riviera. Only there, I had friends, and all kinds of warmth and sunshine. And sailor boys down on the beach.

(She opens her journal again and begins to sing the French folksong, "IL ETAIT UN PETIT NAVIER.")

"IL ÉTAIT UN PETIT NAVIRE.
IL ÉTAIT UN PETIT NAVIRE.
QUI N'AVAIT JA-JA-JAMAIS NAVIGUÉ.
QUI N'AVAIT JA-JA-JAMAIS NAVIGUÉ."

(short beat)

And of course, "mon grand amour," Captain Eduard Josanne.

(She smiles a brief funny smile, which disappears quickly.)

But no "amour" at all from Scott. He was always too busy.

*(**SCOTT** enters holding his unfinished manuscript.)*

SCOTT. God Damn this to Hell.

ZELDA. I don't understand why your work's so immobilized.

SCOTT. If I could find words to explain, I wouldn't be stuck.

ZELDA. At least come down to the beach. The whole gang will be there.

SCOTT. Another time, Baby. I need these pages to fit in the way they're supposed to.

ZELDA. You are such a broken record. A broken record. Broken...

(Mechanically, she picks lint off of his sleeve.)

(a beat)

ZELDA. Darling Heart, do you know why I paint maps on the garden furniture? It's for when you only need your work and Scottie only needs her Nanny and there's no one left needing me...except for Eduard.

SCOTT. Don't you mention that Frog to me.

(She tears herself away from her thought.)

ZELDA. I'm going down on the sand. I need to take in some real warmth, for a change.

*(**ZELDA** grabs her Journal and moves to the "beach." She sits on the sand and tries to sun herself. Although her confidence is shaken, she takes up her Journal, again, and begins to work.)*

*(**SCOTT** transforms into **EDUARD JOSANNE**.)*

EDUARD JOSANNE. Et voila! I thought I would find you here, ma Cherie.

(He shakes his hair, getting her wet.)

ZELDA. Eduard! Watch out! You're soaked, and that water is ice!

EDUARD JOSANNE. Mais oui! But this water is...how do you say it? "Bracing"!

ZELDA. "Bracing" is good. Keeps you alive. Energetic!

EDUARD JOSANNE. You are alone?

ZELDA. Aren't I always?

EDUARD JOSANNE. Where's the little one?

ZELDA. Scottie or Scott?

EDUARD JOSANNE. Be serious, ma Cherie.

ZELDA. You prefer me like that don't you, mon Capitain.

(being very serious)

Scottie's walking with Mamzelle.

EDUARD JOSANNE. Along zee promenade?

ZELDA. Or into town, to buy a sweet. Or maybe to a circus.

EDUARD JOSANNE. *(incredulous)* You really do not know?

ZELDA. Should I?

EDUARD JOSANNE. Well, you are zee Maman.

ZELDA. In name.

EDUARD JOSANNE. You could be more.

ZELDA. I had hoped, but, unfortunately, no. My husband's expectations and social position preclude me from that pleasure.

(He takes her chin in his hand and looks at her sympathetically.)

You look into the very depths of my very being. And wonder of wonders? You find me acceptable.

(He kisses her tenderly on the eyes. A beat.)

EDUARD JOSANNE. Let's go for a swim! Allez-y!

(He pulls her to her feet.)

ZELDA. *(teasing)* The current's not too fast or the tide too high? Scott's afraid of high tide, you know. And of swimming naked anytime at all!

EDUARD JOSANNE. And you, ma Cherie? Are you, too, afraid of such things?

ZELDA. Are you kidding? I like nothing better.

EDUARD JOSANNE. How terrible, Cherie. To have to spend your life with someone so "incompatibile."

ZELDA. Scott? Incompatible? God, wouldn't that be a bitch! If all of this time I've been blinded by him.

EDUARD JOSANNE. Come swim.

ZELDA. No, wait. I need to show you something. Only don't touch. You're wet.

*(**ZELDA** gets out her Journal. She opens it for him to see, but does not hand it to him.)*

Well?

(She turns the pages of the book for him. He becomes more and more enthralled.)

EDUARD JOSANNE. Mon Dieu!

(He indicates that she should keep turning pages.)

EDUARD JOSANNE. These sketches...

> *(pronounced in French)*

> "Formidable"!

ZELDA. She's a dancer.

EDUARD JOSANNE. How you've captured her muscular feet!

ZELDA. She looks exactly how you feel afterwards.

EDUARD JOSANNE. And zee way that you exaggerate her limbs!

ZELDA. All feet and arms and legs.

EDUARD JOSANNE. She is magnifique.

ZELDA. Merci.

EDUARD JOSANNE. And zee polish on her nails! Exactly your color.

> *(ZELDA looks at her hands.)*

ZELDA. You noticed.

EDUARD JOSANNE. Your delicious hands! Drive me wild.

> *(He holds her hands lightly and kisses them.)*

> You are this dancer, non?

ZELDA. Maybe. Once upon a time.

> *(She closes the journal and puts it aside carefully.)*

> I studied with Diaghilev's dance "directrice."

EDUARD JOSANNE. You must be very good.

ZELDA. She believed in me.

EDUARD JOSANNE. Cherie?

ZELDA. She believed in me, and then I let her down. I am such a disappointment. Such a waste of time and money and endless plies!

> *(ZELDA clearly is distressed.)*

> *(EDUARD morphs into MME. EGOROVA with a shift in voice and posture, but no change in costume.)*

EDUARD. *(in MME. EGOROVA's voice)* It will be alright, Daragousha.

(Lights and sound begin to shift.)

ZELDA. Daragousha?

EDUARD. *(in* **MME. EGOROVA**'s *voice)* Time is difficult challenge for artist to be embracing. Let your art be what revives you…what lets you continue.

ZELDA. Madame? I don't understand, I…

EDUARD. *(in* **MME. EGOROVA**'s *voice)* Give permission for your art to let you live.

*(***EDUARD/MME. EGOROVA** *is gone.* **ZELDA** *takes a moment to try and make sense of what has just happened.)*

ZELDA. Give permission for your art to let you live? Of course. Of course! I have to write that down before I forget it. And inscribe Madame's name beneath it… for inspiration.

*(***ZELDA** *retrieves her journal and starts to write.)*

Give permission for your art…

*(***BAR MAN** *enters with his fresh pail of water. He mops the floor.)*

(As **ZELDA** *continues to write, she addresses the* **BAR MAN**.*)*

She was right, you know.

BAR MAN. Who?

ZELDA. So long as the work is only about "yourself"? It winds up being held hostage. Unable to break free. And all because you're scared that once it's out there? It might get laughed at. Ridiculed.

BAR MAN. Even worse…ignored.

ZELDA. I knew we were kindred spirits, Jelly Bean.

BAR MAN. Maybe so. Maybe not.

ZELDA. I'm only trying to help!

BAR MAN. Help me or yourself?

ZELDA. I care too much is all. For Scott…for you…

BAR MAN. Not for me. Just for Scott. He's your husband.

ZELDA. Of course he's my one and only. Although, sometimes? I secretly wish that we had never married.

BAR MAN. You don't really believe that, do you?

ZELDA. *(covering)* Just joking. Just joking, Sugar. Hell. How could I not have married with F. Scott Fitzgerald? He was the only important thing I ever chose. In my whole damned life…for me, you know? So we could get away together…so I wouldn't have to live where my demon could find me.

(The words tumble out.)

Only then I find out, Scott has demons of his own! Like every true artist worth salt. But between his, and mine, and his blockages and boozing…

*(**ZELDA** starts to become overwhelmed again. She picks at some imperfections on her clothing.)*

BAR MAN. Stop scratching.

ZELDA. Can't help it.

BAR MAN. *(He gently restrains her.)* Hey, hey. Easy. Poor kid.

ZELDA. The only "poor kid" that I know is my baby, Scottie. My only appreciative audience now a-days. Unless, of course, you count my fans in the day room. Those dear lost souls will embrace just any ol' thing. So long as it can add color to their white-walled existence.

BAR MAN. Your work makes a difference to them.

(She releases herself from his hold.)

ZELDA. You're right, of course. I should thank my stars *someone* still thinks I'm Mary Cassatt…and Jane Austen and Josephine Baker rolled into one.

(A beat. She goes back to her journal, only this time, she starts sketching.)

I have to keep on working is all. That's the key, isn't it, Jelly Bean? If I ever hope to be worthy of my perfect rose!

*(**ZELDA** sketches with a vengeance.)*

(BAR MAN puts the mop away.)

(ZELDA stops her sketching abruptly.)

Oh, dear. Oh, dear me. I've drawn my very own eyes. Only I've captured them truly this time...for the very first time!

(BAR MAN transforms into SCOTT.)

SCOTT. You've captured what, Minnie Mouse?

ZELDA. My spirit. Look, Scott. I'm changed.

(She hands him her writing journal. Almost in a daze, she touches her face and neck.)

No more tension lines at the mouth. No more eczema scabs on my neck.

SCOTT. Which is why you've signed yourself out?

(ZELDA smiles radiantly.)

ZELDA. Why I'm going to marry with him.

SCOTT. Marry who?

ZELDA. Eduard Josanne.

(a beat)

SCOTT. You are already married. To me.

ZELDA. I need a man who appreciates what I offer.

SCOTT. Your Frog really wants you? Or is this another pipe dream?

ZELDA. You're suggesting I'd manufacture...!

SCOTT. When you get "intent," Baby, anything's possible.

ZELDA. How dare you!

SCOTT. If the Frog wants you let him ask me himself. To my face.

ZELDA. And if he won't?

SCOTT. If he won't, then this affair of yours is a fiction. It only exists in your head.

ZELDA. Scott, I need a divorce.

SCOTT. This is just like your doctor says. You'll never be fixed. Not completely.

ZELDA. With or without approval…I'm going to fly.

(**SCOTT** *grabs* **ZELDA** *by the arm.*)

SCOTT. Not without me, you won't.

ZELDA. Scott! Let go! Darling, please.

(*By now,* **SCOTT** *has grabbed onto both of her arms, which he holds, near her wrists, by the sleeves of her jacket. As* **ZELDA** *backs up, the sleeves elongate…pulled out into "water sleeves" which seem to grow to a length of many feet.* **ZELDA** *panics.*)

My arms! Scott! For God's sake, let go of me!

SCOTT. How can I? We're joined at the hip and the heart!

ZELDA. How can I soar, if you're holding me down so tightly?

SCOTT. Forever and ever…

ZELDA. *(screaming)* God damn it! Let me loose!

(**SCOTT** *releases her. The sleeves now float freely, trailing along the ground, covering* **ZELDA**'s *arms completely.*)

My hands! You've kept my hands!

(*She sinks down to the floor and wails.*)

How could you, Scott! I need my hands…to paint, to write, to express.

(*As she puts her hands to her eyes, she realizes she still has her hands.*)

Wait…they're here.

(*She explores the sleeves, rediscovering her hands. A mixture of relief and embarrassment floods her face.*)

They're where they belong…

(*Furiously, she tears off the extra fabric, which comprises the extensions of her sleeves. She throws the sleeve extensions onto the floor and raises her fists exultantly.*)

…as was always and forever intended!

(*She notices* **SCOTT** *looking at her.*)

If you can't bear to see me clear eyed and upright, then maybe it's your turn to spend time inside, Darling Heart.

(**SCOTT** *exits.*)

(**ZELDA** *leans on the bar. The effort of freeing herself from* **SCOTT** *has left her exhausted.*)

(*She hears music playing. It is the music from Gisele she was to have danced to in her debut.*)

(*As the music washes over her, she follows it. She takes center stage…as the self-assured dancer she was when given her contract. She dances beautifully to this music from* Gisele. *[Playwright's Note: This is* **ZELDA***'s professional ballet debut…or at least, the suggestion of it.]*)

(**BAR MAN** *re-enters the scene. He watches her for a beat, and is enthralled. He sits at the piano and plays to accompany her through her last sequence of turns.* **ZELDA** *ends in a deep and gracious ballet curtsey.*)

(*a beat*)

BAR MAN. You truly are a vision, Zelda.

(**BAR MAN** *gets* **ZELDA***'s journal and hands it to her.*)

ZELDA. Thank you, Piano Man. For taking the time to listen.

(*quietly*)

I'm ready to leave, now.

BAR MAN. Where to?

ZELDA. Why, back inside, I suppose, to my sanctuary. My home away from home, where this spirit can flower.

BAR MAN. Where you'll get your perfect rose?

ZELDA. Where my work has the best chance to flourish and to blossom!

(*a beat*)

And what about you, Sugarplum?

BAR MAN. To bed, I suppose.

ZELDA. Your own?

BAR MAN. Yeah. Relax. I've already got me a runway for launching my music. Every Monday night right here, from eight until close.

ZELDA. Glad to hear that, Jelly Bean. Makes me feel… satisfied.

(She moves to put her coat on.)

I can get you the name of a guy who copies music. I trust him. He works for Paul Whiteman. You interested?

BAR MAN. For protection? Why not!

ZELDA. I'll send around his number.

(She swoops her evening shawl around her body. It drapes her shoulders and hangs down over her back. On this shawl is embroidered a single perfect rose.)

BAR MAN. Hey! You've had that there all along!

ZELDA. *(with a wink)* Why so I have, Jelly Bean! Fancy that.

(She blows him a kiss.)

Fancy that!

(She exits.)

(BAR MAN takes one last look around to make sure all is put away. He discovers an actual perfect rose that ZELDA has left him.)

(He puts the rose on the piano and sits down to fool with the bass line and chord combination we heard before.)

(As he plays working on this tune of his own creation, the lights fade.)

End of Play

www.ingramcontent.com/pod-product-compliance
Lightning Source LLC
Chambersburg PA
CBHW070417120726
47909CB00005B/1681